A Classic
Treasury of
Nursery Songs
& Rhymes

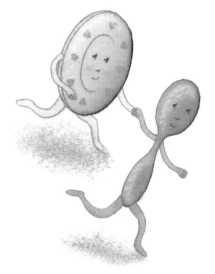

A Classic Treasury of Nursery Songs & Rhymes

Illustrated by Tracey Moroney

The Five Mile Press

The Five Mile Press

The Five Mile Press Pty Ltd
950 Stud Road, Rowville
Victoria 3178 Australia
Email: publishing@fivemile.com.au
Website: www.fivemile.com.au

This edition first published 2002
Reprinted in 2003 (three times), 2004 (four times), 2005

Illustrations © Tracey Moroney
CD produced by Stephanie Mann, recorded at Spoken Word Productions
This collection © The Five Mile Press Pty Ltd

Printed in China

National Library of Australia
Cataloguing-in-Publication data
A classic treasury of nursery songs and rhymes

ISBN 1 86503 696 X

1. Nursery rhymes, English. 2. Children's poetry, English. 3. Children's songs -
Texts
398.8

CONTENTS

The first verses and songs children learn
are never forgotten. They form a rich part of a
child's literary heritage, helping to inspire a love
of language — with their simple rhythms and
rhymes. As the creators of these traditional nursery
rhymes and songs seemed to instinctively know,
small children love repetition – possibly because it
helps them to learn new words.

Since time immemorial, parents have been reciting
or singing verses to their children. Many of the
oldest rhymes in this collection have been passed
on, down the generations, from parent to child. And
one day, the young readers of this book may in turn
pass these rhymes on to their own children.

Hickory, Dickory, Dock

Hickory, dickory, dock,
The mouse ran up the clock.
The clock struck one,
The mouse ran down,
Hickory, dickory, dock!

THE WHEELS ON THE BUS

The wheels on the bus go round and round,
Round and round, round and round!
The wheels on the bus go round and round,
All over town.

The doors on the bus swing open and shut,
Open and shut, open and shut!
The doors on the bus swing open and shut,
All over town.

The wiper on the bus goes swish, swish, swish,
Swish, swish, swish,
Swish, swish, swish!
The wiper on the bus goes
Swish, swish, swish,
All over town.

The people on the bus go bump, bump, bump,
Bump, bump, bump,
Bump, bump, bump!
The people on the bus go bump, bump, bump,
All over town.

*L*ITTLE BOY BLUE

Little boy blue,
Come blow your horn,
The sheep's in the meadow,
The cow's in the corn.
Where's the boy
That looks after the sheep?
He's in the haystack,
Fast asleep.

HERE WE GO ROUND
THE MULBERRY BUSH

Here we go round the mulberry bush,
The mulberry bush, the mulberry bush,
Here we go round the mulberry bush,
On a cold and frosty morning.

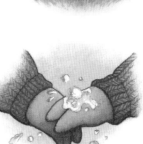

This is the way we wash our hands,
Wash our hands, wash our hands,
This is the way we wash our hands,
On a cold and frosty morning.

This is the way we go to school,
Go to school, go to school,
This is the way we go to school,
On a cold and frosty morning.

BAA, BAA, BLACK SHEEP

Baa, baa, black sheep,
Have you any wool?
Yes sir, yes sir,
Three bags full.
One for the master,
One for the dame,
And one for the little boy
Who lives down the lane.

If you're happy and you know it

If you're happy and you know it,
Clap your hands,
If you're happy and you know it,
Clap your hands,
If you're happy and you know it,
Then you should surely show it,
If you're happy and you know it,
CLAP YOUR HANDS!

If you're happy and you know it,
Stamp your feet,
If you're happy and you know it,
Stamp your feet,
If you're happy and you know it,
Then you should surely show it,
If you're happy and you know it,
STAMP YOUR FEET!

If you're happy and you know it,
Jump around,
If you're happy and you know it,
Jump around,
If you're happy and you know it,
Then you should surely show it,
If you're happy and you know it,
JUMP AROUND!

ANIMAL FAIR

I went to animal fair,
The birds and beasts were there,
The big baboon by the light of the moon,
Was combing his auburn hair.
The monkey, he got drunk,
And slid down the elephant's trunk,
The elephant sneezed and fell to his knees,
But what became of the monkey,
Monkey, monkey, monk?

OLD MACDONALD

Old MacDonald had a farm,
E-I-E-I-O,
And on that farm he had some ducks,
E-I-E-I-O,
With a quack-quack here and a quack-quack there,
Here a quack, there a quack, everywhere a quack-quack.
Old MacDonald had a farm,
E-I-E-I-O.

Old MacDonald had a farm,
E-I-E-I-O,
And on that farm he had some cows,
E-I-E-I-O,
With a moo-moo here and a moo-moo there,
Here a moo, there a moo, everywhere a moo-moo.
Old MacDonald had a farm,
E-I-E-I-O.

Old MacDonald had a farm,
E-I-E-I-O,
And on that farm he had some pigs,
E-I-E-I-O,
With an oink-oink here and an oink-oink there,
Here an oink, there an oink, everywhere an oink-oink.
Old MacDonald had a farm,
E-I-E-I-O.

Old MacDonald had a farm,
E-I-E-I-O,
And on that farm he had some sheep,
E-I-E-I-O,
With a baa-baa here, and a baa-baa there,
Here a baa, there a baa, everywhere a baa-baa.
Old MacDonald had a farm,
E-I-E-I-O.

THE OWL AND THE PUSSY CAT

The owl and the pussy cat went to sea
In a beautiful pea-green boat,
They took some honey and plenty of money,
Wrapped up in a five pound note.
The owl looked up to the stars above,
And sang to a small guitar,
"Oh, lovely Pussy! Oh, Pussy, my love,
What a beautiful pussy you are, you are!
What a beautiful pussy you are!"

Pussy said to the owl, "You elegant fowl!
How charmingly sweet you sing!
Oh, let us be married! Too long we have tarried,
But what shall we do for a ring?"
They sailed away for a year and a day,
To the land where the Bong-tree grows,
And there in a wood a piggy-wig stood,
With a ring at the end of his nose, his nose,
With a ring at the end of his nose.

"Dear Pig, are you willing to sell for one shilling
Your ring?" Said the piggy, "I will."
So they took it away and were married next day
By the turkey who lives on the hill.
They dined on mince and slices of quince,
Which they ate with a runcible spoon.
And hand in hand, on the edge of the sand,
They danced by the light of the moon,
They danced by the light of the moon.

Edward Lear

ONE, TWO, THREE, FOUR, FIVE

One, two, three, four, five,
Once I caught a fish alive.

Six, seven, eight, nine, ten,
Then I let it go again.

Why did you let it go?
Because it bit my finger so.
Which finger did it bite?
This little finger on my right.

POP! GOES THE WEASEL

All around the cobbler's bench,
The monkey chased the weasel.
The monkey thought 'twas all in fun.
Pop! goes the weasel.
A penny for a spool of thread,
A penny for a needle,
That's the way the money goes.
Pop! goes the weasel.

Row, row, ROW YOUR BOAT

Row, row, row your boat
Gently down the stream,
Merrily, merrily, merrily, merrily
Life is but a dream.

DOWN AT THE STATION

Down at the station, early in the morning,
See the little puffer-billies all in a row.
See the engine-driver pull his little lever —
PUFF-PUFF! PEEP-PEEP!
Off we go!

IT'S RAINING, IT'S POURING

It's raining, it's pouring,
The old man's snoring,
He bumped his head
Upon the bed,
And he couldn't get up in the morning.

TWINKLE, TWINKLE LITTLE STAR

Twinkle, twinkle, little star,
How I wonder what you are,
Up above the world so high,
Like a diamond in the sky.
Twinkle, twinkle, little star,
How I wonder what you are!

THE FARMER IN THE DELL

The farmer in the dell,
The farmer in the dell,
Heigh-ho, the dairy-o,
The farmer in the dell.

The farmer takes a wife,
The farmer takes a wife,
Heigh-ho, the dairy-o,
The farmer takes a wife.

The wife takes a child,
The wife takes a child,
Heigh-ho, the dairy-o,
The wife takes a child.

The child takes a cat,
The child takes a cat,
Heigh-ho, the dairy-o,
The child takes a cat.

The cat takes a mouse,
The cat takes a mouse,
Heigh-ho, the dairy-o,
The cat takes a mouse.

The mouse takes the cheese,
The mouse takes the cheese,
Heigh-ho, the dairy-o,
The mouse takes the cheese.

They all run after the cheese,
They all run after the cheese,
Heigh-ho, the dairy-o,
They all run after the cheese.

THE OTHER DAY I MET A BEAR

The other day, the other day,
I met a bear, I met a bear,
Out in the woods away out there.
I met a bear, I met a bear,
Out in the woods away out there.

He looked at me, he looked at me,
I looked at him, I looked at him,
He sized up me, I sized up him.
He looked at me, he looked at me,
I looked at him, I looked at him.
He sized up me, I sized up him.

He said to me, he said to me,
"Why don't you run? Why don't you run?
* I see you don't have any gun."

I said to him, I said to him,
"That's a good idea, that's a good idea.
Come on now, feet, get out of here."

And so I ran, and so I ran
Away from there, away from there,
But right behind me came that bear.

And then I saw, and then I saw
Ahead of me, ahead of me
A great big tree, oh, glory be!

The lowest branch, the lowest branch
Was ten feet up, was ten feet up
I'd have to jump and trust my luck.

And so I jumped, and so I jumped
Into the air, into the air
But missed the branch away up there.

But don't you fret, but don't you fret
And don't you frown, and don't you frown,
I caught that branch on the way down.

That's all there is, that's all there is,
There ain't no more, there ain't no more
Unless I see that bear once more.

* In verses 3 to 10, repeat the last line

LAVENDER'S BLUE

Lavender's blue, diddle, diddle,
Lavender's green;
When I am king, diddle, diddle,
You shall be queen.

Roses are red, diddle, diddle,
Violets are blue,
Because you love me, diddle, diddle,
I will love you.

Let the birds sing, diddle, diddle,
And the lambs play,
We shall be safe, diddle, diddle,
Out of harm's way.

THE GRAND OLD DUKE OF YORK

Oh the grand old Duke of York,
He had ten thousand men.
He marched them up to the top of the hill,
And he marched them down again.
And when they were up, they were up,
And when they were down, they were down,
And when they were only half-way up,
They were neither up nor down.

THE HOKEY POKEY

You put your right hand in,
You put your right hand out,
You put your right hand in,
And you shake it all about.

chorus
You do the hokey-pokey
And you turn around,
That's what it's all about!

You put your left hand in,
You put your left hand out,
You put your left hand in,
And you shake it all about.

You put your right foot in,
You put your right foot out,
You put your right foot in,
And you shake it all about.

You put your left foot in,
You put your left foot out,
You put your left foot in,
And you shake it all about.

You put your whole self in,
You put your whole self out,
You put your whole self in,
And you shake it all about.

FIVE LITTLE DUCKS

Five little ducks
Went out to play,
Over the hills and far away,
Mother duck said,
Quack, quack, quack, quack,
But only *four* little ducks came back.

Four little ducks
Went out to play,
Over the hills and far away,
Mother duck said,
Quack, quack, quack, quack,
But only *three* little ducks came back.

Three little ducks
Went out to play,
Over the hills and far away,
Mother duck said,
Quack, quack, quack, quack,
But only *two* little ducks came back.

Two little ducks
Went out to play,
Over the hills and far away,
Mother duck said,
Quack, quack, quack, quack,
But only *one* little duck came back.

One little duck went out to play,
Over the hills and far away,
Mother duck said,
Quack, quack, quack, quack,
And all of the *five* little ducks came back!

MISS POLLY'S DOLLY

Miss Polly had a dolly
Who was sick, sick, sick,
So she called for the doctor
To be quick, quick, quick.

The doctor came
With his bag and hat,
And he knocked on the door
With a rat-a-tat-tat.

He looked at the dolly
And he shook his head,
And he said, "Miss Polly,
Put her straight to bed."

He wrote on a paper
For a pill, pill, pill,
"I'll be back in
  the morning,
With my bill, bill, bill."

HOT CROSS BUNS

Hot cross buns, hot cross buns,
One a penny, two a penny,
Hot cross buns.

If you have no daughters,
Give them to your sons,
One a penny, two a penny,
Hot cross buns.

SING A SONG OF SIXPENCE

Sing a song of sixpence,
A pocket full of rye;
Four-and-twenty blackbirds
Baked in a pie.

When the pie was opened,
The birds began to sing;
Oh, wasn't that a dainty dish
To set before a king!

THE BEAR WENT OVER THE MOUNTAIN

The bear went over the mountain,
The bear went over the mountain,
The bear went over the mountain,
To see what he could see,
To see what he could see,
To see what he could see,
The bear went over the mountain
To see what he could see.

The bear went over the mountain,
The bear went over the mountain,
The bear went over the mountain,
And what do you think he saw?
And what do you think he saw?
And what do you think he saw?
The bear went over the mountain
And what do you think he saw?

The other side of the mountain,
The other side of the mountain,
The other side of the mountain,
Was all that he could see,
Was all that he could see,
Was all that he could see,
The other side of the mountain
Was all that he could see.

ORANGES AND LEMONS

Oranges and lemons, say the bells of St Clements.
You owe me five farthings, say the bells of St Martins.
When will you pay me? say the bells of Old Bailey.
When I grow rich, say the bells of Shoreditch.
When will that be? say the bells of Stepney.
I'm sure I don't know, says the Great Bell of Bow.
Here comes a candle to light you to bed.
And here comes a chopper to chop off your head!

Noah's Ark

The animals all went into the ark,
Hurrah, hurrah!
The animals all went into the ark,
Hurrah, hurrah!
The animals went in two by two,
The elephant and the kangaroo,
They all went into the ark,
To get in, out of the rain.

OH WHERE, OH WHERE HAS MY LITTLE DOG GONE?

Oh where, oh where has my little dog gone?
Oh where, oh where can he be?
With his ears cut short and his tail cut long,
Oh where, oh where can he be?

FIVE LITTLE MONKEYS

Five little monkeys bouncing on the bed,
One fell off and bumped his head,
Mamma called the doctor and the doctor said,
"No more monkey business bouncing on the bed!"

Four little monkeys bouncing on the bed,
One fell off and bumped his head,
Mamma called the doctor and the doctor said,
"No more monkey business bouncing on the bed!"

Three little monkeys bouncing on the bed,
One fell off and bumped his head,
Mamma called the doctor and the doctor said,
"No more monkey business bouncing on the bed!"

Two little monkeys bouncing on the bed,
One fell off and bumped his head,
Mamma called the doctor and the doctor said,
"No more monkey business bouncing on the bed!"

One little monkey bouncing on the bed,
One fell off and bumped his head,
Mamma called the doctor and the doctor said,
(you guessed it!) "NO MORE MONKEY
BUSINESS BOUNCING ON THE BED!"

THE TWELVE DAYS OF CHRISTMAS

On the first day of Christmas
My true love sent to me
A partridge in a pear tree.

On the second day of Christmas
My true love sent to me
Two turtle doves,
And a partridge in a pear tree.

On the third day of Christmas
My true love sent to me
Three French hens,
Two turtle doves,
And a partridge in a pear tree.

On the fourth day of Christmas
My true love sent to me
Four calling birds,
Three French hens,
Two turtle doves,
And a partridge in a pear tree.

On the fifth day of Christmas
My true love sent to me
Five gold rings,
Four calling birds,
Three French hens,
Two turtle doves,
And a partridge in a pear tree.

On the sixth day of Christmas
My true love sent to me
Six geese a-laying,
Five gold rings,
Four calling birds,
Three French hens,
Two turtle doves,
And a partridge in a pear tree.

On the seventh day of Christmas
My true love sent to me
Seven swans a-swimming,
Six geese a-laying,
Five gold rings,
Four calling birds,
Three French hens,
Two turtle doves,
And a partridge in a pear tree.

On the eighth day of Christmas
My true love sent to me
Eight maids a-milking,
Seven swans a-swimming,
Six geese a-laying,
Five gold rings,
Four calling birds,
Three French hens,
Two turtle doves,
And a partridge in a pear tree.

On the ninth day of Christmas
My true love sent to me
Nine drummers drumming,
Eight maids a-milking,
Seven swans a-swimming,
Six geese a-laying,
Five gold rings,
Four calling birds,
Three French hens,
Two turtle doves,
And a partridge in a pear tree.

On the tenth day of Christmas
My true love sent to me
Ten pipers piping,
Nine drummers drumming,
Eight maids a-milking,
Seven swans a-swimming,
Six geese a-laying,
Five gold rings,
Four calling birds,
Three French hens,
Two turtle doves,
And a partridge in a pear tree.

On the eleventh day of Christmas
My true love sent to me
Eleven ladies dancing,
Ten pipers piping,
Nine drummers drumming,
Eight maids a-milking,
Seven swans a-swimming,
Six geese a-laying,
Five gold rings,
Four calling birds,
Three French hens,
Two turtle doves,
And a partridge in a pear tree.

On the twelfth day of Christmas
My true love sent to me
Twelve lords a-leaping,
Eleven ladies dancing,
Ten pipers piping,
Nine drummers drumming,
Eight maids a-milking,
Seven swans a-swimming,
Six geese a-laying,
Five gold rings,
Four calling birds,
Three French hens,
Two turtle doves,
And a partridge in a pear tree.

I SAW THREE SHIPS A-SAILING

I saw three ships come sailing by,
Come sailing by, come sailing by,
I saw three ships come sailing by,
On Christmas Day, in the morning.

And what do you think was in them then,
Was in them then, was in them then?
And what do you think was in them then,
On Christmas Day, in the morning?

Three pretty girls were in them then,
Were in them then, were in them then;
Three pretty girls were in them then,
On Christmas Day, in the morning.

And one could whistle,
  and one could sing,
And one could play on the violin —
Such joy there was at my wedding,
On Christmas Day, in the morning.

JINGLE BELLS

Jingle bells, jingle bells,
Jingle all the way,
Hurrah for dear old Santa Claus,
Hurrah for Christmas Day!

JACK BE NIMBLE

Jack be nimble,
Jack be quick,
Jack jump over
The candlestick.

SEE-SAW, MARGERY DAW

See-saw, Margery Daw,
Jacky shall have a new master.
Jacky shall have but a penny a day
Because he can't go any faster.

JACK & JILL

Jack and Jill went up the hill
To fetch a pail of water.
Jack fell down and broke his crown,
And Jill came tumbling after.

Up Jack got, and home did trot,
As fast as he could caper.
He went to bed to mend his head,
With vinegar and brown paper.

PUSSY CAT, PUSSY CAT

Pussy cat, pussy cat, where have you been?
I've been to London to visit the queen.
Pussy cat, pussy cat, what did you there?
I frightened a little mouse under her chair.

OLD KING COLE

Old King Cole
Was a merry old soul,
And a merry old soul was he.
He called for his pipe,
And he called for his bowl,
And he called for his fiddlers three.

THE LION AND THE UNICORN

The lion and the unicorn
Were fighting for the crown;
The lion beat the unicorn
All around the town.

Some gave them white bread,
And some gave them brown;
Some gave them plum cake
And drummed them
   out of town.

THE CROCODILE

If you should meet a crocodile
Don't take a stick and poke him;
Ignore the welcome in his smile,
Be careful not to stroke him.
For as he sleeps upon the Nile,
He thinner gets and thinner;
But when'er you meet a crocodile
He's ready for his dinner.

THREE LITTLE KITTENS

Three little kittens they lost their mittens,
And they began to cry,
"Oh! Mother dear, we greatly fear
Our mittens we have lost."

"What! Lost your mittens,
You naughty kittens,
Then you shall have no pie.
Mee-ow, mee-ow, mee-ow.
Then you shall have no pie."

Three little kittens they found their mittens,
And they began to cry,
"Oh! Mother dear,
See here, see here,
Our mittens we have found."

"What! Found your mittens,
You good little kittens,
Then you shall have some pie.
Purr, purr, purr.
Yes, you shall have some pie."

The three little kittens put on their mittens,
And soon ate up the pie;
"Oh! Mother dear,
We greatly fear,
Our mittens we have soiled."

"What! Soiled your mittens,
You naughty kittens,"
Then they began to sigh,
"Mee-ow, mee-ow, mee-ow."
Then they began to sigh.

The three little kittens
They washed their mittens,
And hung them out to dry;
"Oh! Mother dear,
See here, see here,
Our mittens we have washed."

"What! Washed your mittens,
You good little kittens!
But I smell a rat close by.
Hush, hush, miew, miew,
I smell a rat close by,
Miew, miew, miew."

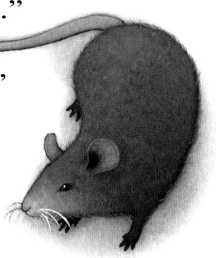

COCK-A-DOODLE-DOO!

Cock-a-doodle-doo!
My dame has lost her shoe;
My master's lost his
  fiddling stick;
And doesn't know what to do.

Cock-a-doodle-doo!
My dame has found her shoe;
My master's found his fiddling stick;
Sing doodle-doodle-doo!

MIX A PANCAKE

Mix a pancake,
Stir a pancake,
Pop it in the pan;
Fry the pancake,
Toss the pancake —
Catch it if you can.

Christina Rossetti

LITTLE TOMMY TUCKER

Little Tommy Tucker
Sings for his supper;
What shall we give him?
White bread and butter.

I SAW A SHIP

I saw a ship a-sailing,
A-sailing on the sea,
And oh, but it was laden
With pretty things for thee!

There were comfits in the cabin,
And apples in the hold;
The sails were made of silk,
And the masts were all of gold.

The four-and-twenty sailors,
That stood between the decks,
Were four-and-twenty white mice
With chains around their necks.

The captain was a duck
With a packet on his back,
And when the ship began to move
The captain said, Quack! Quack!

TEDDY BEAR, TEDDY BEAR

Teddy bear, teddy bear, run upstairs,

Teddy bear, teddy bear, say your prayers.

Teddy bear, teddy bear, turn out the light,

Teddy bear, teddy bear, say good-night!

HEY DIDDLE, DIDDLE

Hey diddle, diddle,
The cat and the fiddle,
The cow jumped over the moon.
The little dog laughed
To see such sport,
And the dish ran away with the spoon.

A WISE OLD OWL

A wise old owl lived
  in an oak.
The more he saw
The less he spoke.
The less he spoke
The more he heard.
Why can't we all be
Like that wise old bird?

RING O'ROSES

Ring-a-ring o' roses,
A pocket full of posies,
A-tishoo! A-tishoo!
We all fall down.

THE QUEEN OF HEARTS

The Queen of Hearts
She made some tarts,
All on a summer's day.
The Knave of Hearts
He stole the tarts,
And took them clean away.
The King of Hearts
Called for the tarts,
And beat the Knave full sore.
The Knave of Hearts
Brought back the tarts,
And vowed he'd steal no more.

HERE WAS AN OLD WOMAN

There was an old woman
Who lived in a shoe,
She had so many children
She didn't know what to do;
She gave them some broth
Without any bread,
And whipped them all soundly
And sent them to bed.

$\mathscr{I}$ HAD A LITTLE NUT TREE

I had a little nut tree,
Nothing would it bear
But a silver nutmeg
And a golden pear.
The king of Spain's daughter
Came to visit me,
And all for the sake
Of my little nut tree.

OLD MOTHER HUBBARD

Old Mother Hubbard
Went to the cupboard
To get her poor dog a bone,
But when she got there
The cupboard was bare,
And so the poor dog had none.

She went to the fishmonger's
To buy him some fish,
But when she came back
He was licking the dish.

She went to the ale-house
To get him some beer,
But when she came back
He sat in a chair.

She went to the tavern
For white wine and red,
But when she came back
He stood on his head.

She went to the fruiterer's
To buy him some fruit,
But when she came back
He was playing the flute.

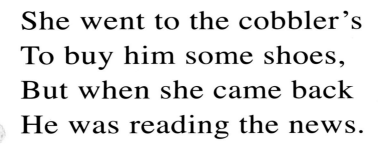

She went to the cobbler's
To buy him some shoes,
But when she came back
He was reading the news.

She went to the hosier's
To buy him some hose,
But when she came back
He was dressed in his clothes.

The dame made a curtsey,
The dog made a bow;
The dame said, "Your servant."
The dog said, "Bow-wow!"

GOOSEY, GOOSEY GANDER

Goosey, goosey, gander
Whither shall I wander?
Upstairs and downstairs
And in my lady's chamber.

There I met an old man
Who wouldn't say his prayers.
I took him by the left leg,
And threw him down the stairs.

Mary, Mary, Quite Contrary

Mary, Mary, quite contrary,
How does your garden grow?
With silver bells and cockle-shells,
And pretty maids all in a row.

Seashells

She sells seashells on the seashore.
The shells that she sells are seashells,
So if she sells seashells on the seashore
I'm sure that the shells
Are seashore seashells.

COBBLER, COBBLER

Cobbler, cobbler, mend my shoe,
Have it done by half-past two.
If it is not done by then,
Have it done by half-past ten.

HODDLEY, PODDLEY

Hoddley, poddley, puddle and fogs,
Cats are to marry the poodle dogs;
Cats in blue jackets
And dogs in red hats,
What will become of the mice
 and rats?

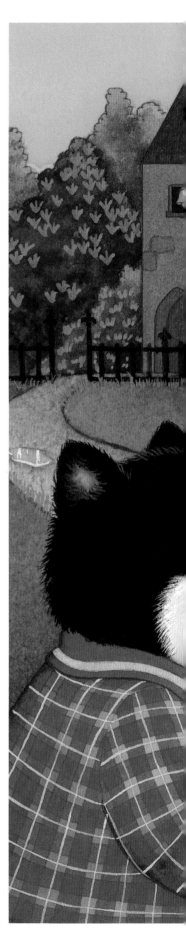

RUB-A-DUB-DUB

Rub-a-dub-dub,
Three men in a tub,
And who do you think they were?
The butcher, the baker,
The candlestick-maker,
All going to the fair.

LITTLE MISS MUFFET

Little Miss Muffet
Sat on a tuffet,
Eating her curds and whey.
Along came a spider
Who sat down beside her
And frightened Miss Muffet away.

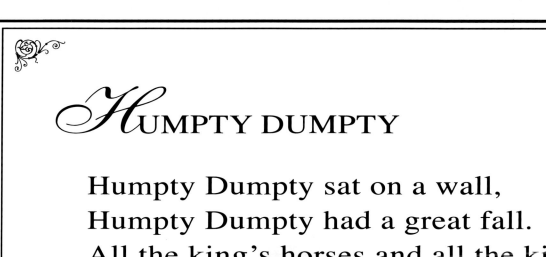

HUMPTY DUMPTY

Humpty Dumpty sat on a wall,
Humpty Dumpty had a great fall.
All the king's horses and all the king's men,
Couldn't put Humpty together again.

POLLY PUT THE KETTLE ON

Polly put the kettle on,
Polly put the kettle on,
Polly put the kettle on,
We'll all have tea.

Sukey take it off again,
Sukey take it off again,
Sukey take it off again,
They've all gone away.

SIX LITTLE MICE

Six little mice sat down to spin.
Pussy passed by and she peeped in.
What are you doing, my little men?
Weaving coats for gentlemen.
Shall I come in and cut off your threads?
No, no, Mistress Pussy,
You'd bite off our heads.
Oh, no, I'll not; I'll help you spin.
That may be so, but you don't come in.

RAIN

Rain on the grass,
And rain on the tree,
Rain on the rooftop,
But not on me!

ONE, TWO BUCKLE MY SHOE

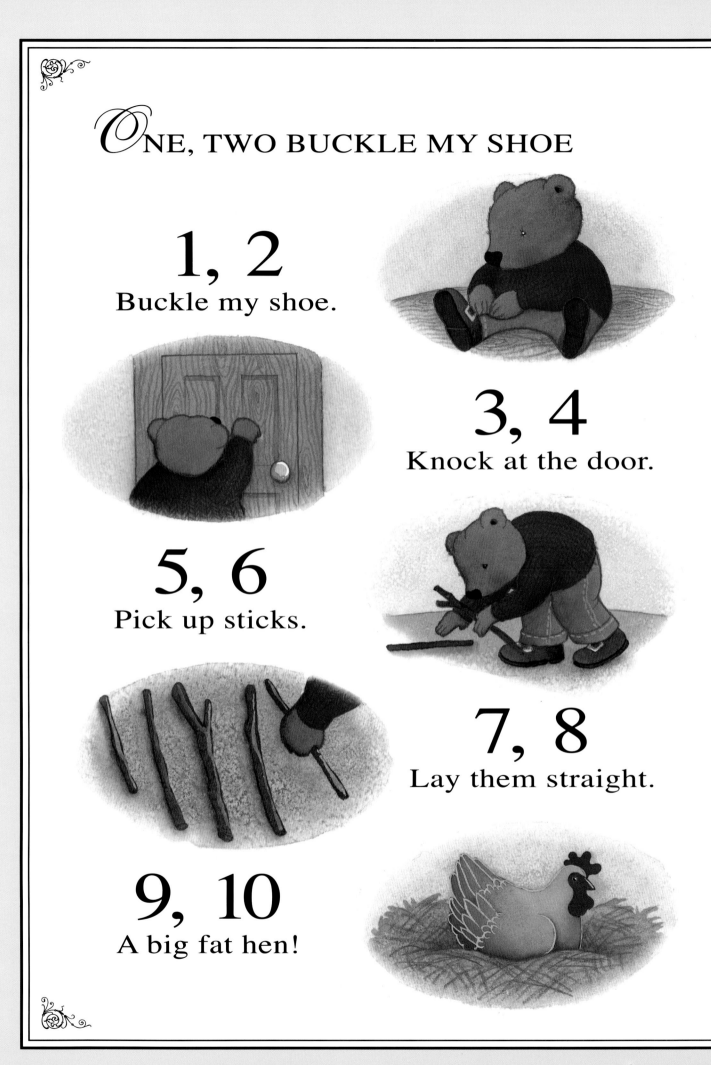

1, 2
Buckle my shoe.

3, 4
Knock at the door.

5, 6
Pick up sticks.

7, 8
Lay them straight.

9, 10
A big fat hen!

11, 12
Dig and delve.

13, 14
Maids a-courting.

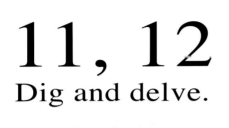

15, 16
Maids in the kitchen.

17, 18
Maids a-waiting.

19, 20
My plate's empty!

HICKETY, PICKETY

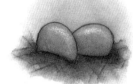

Hickety, pickety, my red hen,
She lays eggs for gentlemen.
Sometimes nine, and sometimes ten,
Hickety, pickety, my red hen.

JACK SPRAT

Jack Sprat could eat no fat,
His wife could eat no lean:
And so betwixt them both, you see,
They lick'd the platter clean.

WEE WILLIE WINKIE

Wee Willie Winkie
Runs through the town,
Upstairs and downstairs in his nightgown,
Rapping at the window,
Crying through the lock,
"Are all the children in their beds?
It's after eight o'clock."

BOYS AND GIRLS

Boys and girls come out to play,
The moon doth shine as bright as day.
Leave your supper and leave your sleep,
And join your playfellows in the street.
Come with a whoop and come with a call,
Come with a good will or not at all.
Up the ladder and over the wall,
A tuppenny loaf will serve us all.

THE MAN IN THE MOON

The Man in the Moon
Looked out of the moon,
Looked out of the moon and said,
"Tis time for all children on earth
To think about getting to bed."

I SEE THE MOON

I see the moon,
And the moon sees me,
God bless the moon,
And God bless me.

STAR LIGHT, STAR BRIGHT

Star light, star bright,
First star I see tonight,
I wish I may, I wish I might
Have the wish I wish tonight.

Goodnight!